Lamar's Story

by Claudia Grande

For now we see through a glass, darkly; but then face to face: now I know in part; but then shall I know even as also I am known.
And now abideth faith, hope, charity, these three; but the greatest of these is charity.
1 Corinthians 13:12-13

First published May 2025. LeGrande Publishing London and Dubai.

CONTENTS

PROLOGUE

Main character

Name: Lamar

Age: 15

Personality: Quiet, observant, carries too much weight on his shoulders, determined but tired

Goal: Keep his grades up and stay invisible

Conflict: Internal (emotional burden) and External (home life, bullying)

Family Situation
Dad: Alcoholic, sometimes gone for days, spends money on drinks or drugs (maybe cocaine/crack). Sometimes violent, unpredictable.

Mom: Party girl, in and out of the house, avoids responsibility, pretends everything is fine to others.

Lamar: Often left alone, does most things himself – cooking, laundry, waking himself up, trying to hide how bad things are.

Teacher (Miss Henry): A black female teacher who sees something in Lamar. Doesn't force him to talk but offers help more than once. She may be the one who reports things.

Bully (Jake): White kid who called Lamar names like 'Crack baby' or 'Gangster'. Comes from a 'better' background but is cruel out of boredom or learned behaviour.

Setting

- Public school (not fancy, but one with decent teachers who try)
- A flat or rundown house in a rough area (sirens at night, gang graffiti, dodgy people around)

CHAPTER 1

The smell hit him first – cheap beer, stale smoke and something else he didn't want to name.

Lamar stepped over his dad's arm, careful not to kick the empty bottle rolling on the carpet. His school shirt was still damp from where he's tried to dry it with the hairdryer last night. There was no milk. No cereal. No clean spoon, even if there was.

Outside, sirens screamed past the window like they were late for something.

He grabbed his bag and closed the front door behind him, quietly, like always. Because waking his dad was a gamble and most mornings, Lamar didn't feel like playing.

Lamar's feet slapped the pavement, fast and hard, like if he ran fast enough he could leave the smell of home behind. The air outside was sharp and his jumper wasn't thick enough. But cold was better than the heat inside – heat that came from rage, rot and whatever his dad had coughed up on the carpet last night.

He didn't eat.

Again.

Didn't even check. The fridge door was held shut with duct tape after the handle broke two months ago and the last time he opened it all he found was one egg and a half empty bottle of hot sauce.

His stomach growled, but he ignored it. He was used to that sound.

CHAPTER 2

The bell rang just as he turned the corner to school. He slipped through the side gate, head down, trying to blend in. Like a ghost.

Missed first period. Again. He'd get told off, maybe a letter sent home – but who'd read it? His mum hadn't opened a letter in weeks.

He crept into the second lesson Maths. Lamar sat at the back and the teacher didn't even pause when he walked in. Lamar was good at that. Being invisible.

" Yo" someone hissed from two rows down. "Your dad get locked up again or what?"

He didn't look up.

The voice laughed. Jake. Of course.

Jake waited until the teacher turned to the whiteboard before flicking a scrunched-up piece of paper straight at Lamar's head. It bounced off his ear.

He ignored it.

Another one came. This time with something scribbled on it:

"Crackhead kid. No wonder you stink."

Lamar swallowed the lump in his throat. His jumper did smell. Musty. He'd pulled it off the radiator still damp this morning.

Jake snickered behind him, whispering something to the girl next to him. She looked at Lamar, then quickly away.

He shrank into his seat. Counted seconds. Prayed for the bell.

In the cafeteria, Lamar walked past the hot meal line. He didn't have the free meal card anymore – his mum never sent in the renewal form. Just another thing she forgot between hangovers and her Friday-night lashes.

He sat at the edge of the dining hall with nothing but a bottle of water he'd filled from the tap at home. His stomach burned.

Jake and his friends walked past, one of them holding a tray piled with food.

"Don't worry mate" Jake said. Voice fake sweet. "You can lick my plate when I'm done."

Lamar looked away.

For the rest of the lunch break Jake's friend group kept looking at him and saying how good the food tasted, meanwhile others laughed and looked at him.

Lamar had had enough and grabbed his bottle of water that by now was half empty and ran out of the dining room and into the bathrooms where he normally goes for every break time at school.

CHAPTER 3

When Lamar got home, the front door was already open a crack.

His dad hadn't moved. Still on the sofa an empty can in his hand, TV flashing blue light across his face. The news was on – some story about a stabbing in the next block.

Lamar stepped in, careful not to trip over the broken table leg that'd been lying in the hallway for a week. The smell was worse now. Like sweat and stale alcohol and sadness.

"Mum?" he called.

No answer.

Just a buzz from her phone left on the counter. Ten missed calls. Two unread messages. One from 'Damo X.'

He didn't bother reading the others.

Later that night, Lamar lay in bed staring at the cracked ceiling. He wore socks to sleep. His toes got cold when the boiler cut out – again.

Somewhere outside, tyres screeched and someone shouted. The silence.

He turned to the wall, pulled the covers tighter and let the tears slide down, quietly. Like always.

CHAPTER 4

The next day the gym was packed.

Rows and rows of students fidgeting, whispering , laughing behind their hands.

Lamar sat near the back, shoulders hunched, eyes fixed on the floor. He hated assemblies.

All that fake energy.

All that noise.

Some head teacher he didn't know was banging on about future goals and careers, waving a slideshow around with pictures of smiling kids in suits.

Lamar's stomach growled again.

He stared at the polished shoes in front of him, imagining what it'd be like to wear ones that didn't pinch his toes.

"Lamar."

His name snapped through the fog.

He looked up. A teacher – Mr Hardy was staring at him. The whole row had turned around. Even Jake.

"Eyes front, please."

Lamar blinked, nodded, mumbled, "Sorry, sir"

The sniggers came a second later.

After assembly, he tried to slip away but Miss Henry caught his arm in the corridor.

"Lamar? You all right?"

He nodded. Too fast.

"You've been late three times this week."

"I know. Sorry. My alarm's... It broke."

She didn't look convinced.

"You eating okay? You're looking pretty thin."

He hesitated.

She clocked the pause.

"Lamar" she said gently, "I'm not trying to get you in trouble. I'm just saying – if there's something going on, you can talk to someone. Me. Or the school counsellor. All right?"

He nodded again. She let go of his arm and Lamar started to walk away. But he didn't look back.

School went past quickly and now he was back home, Lamar found an old photo on the floor by the kitchen table. It was bent at the corners, slightly sticky.

It was of him and his parents – before. Before the shouting. Before the bottles.

His dad had both arms around them, laughing. His mum had her hair tied up and was actually smiling, not that fake kind she used now when she was pretending to be fine.

Lamar stared at it for a long time. Wishing that he could go back to that time in his life.

Back when they were a family.

The front door slammed just before midnight. Lamar shot up in bed, heart racing.

He grabbed his duvet and listened to the sounds coming from the front of the house.

He heard her heels first. Then a laugh. Then silence.

He waited until the hallway light flicked off before creeping out.

She was in the kitchen, rummaging for crisps or something.

"Mum?" he whispered.

She turned around too fast. Smelled like vodka and fake flowers.

“Jesus, Lamar – don’t sneak up on people like that” she snapped. “What are you doing up?”

“I thought...”

“You think too much,” she said cutting him off. “Go to bed.”

He stared at her for a moment. She wouldn’t meet his eyes.

Then she poured herself another drink.

Lamar walks back to his room. Looking down to the floor. He got to his room and went to close the door behind him. He could see his mom drinking another drink and saying things about dad that he couldn’t make out through her delayed speech.

At that moment while he was preparing to go back to sleep, he wished that he could go back to live in the moment that photo was taken.

CHAPTER 5

Next day. Lamar was trying to sleep off another empty stomach when a banging at the door made him jump.

His dad groaned from the sofa.

The knocking didn't stop.

BANG. BANG. BANG.

"Open the door, Mr Brown. It's the police."

Lamar's heart forgot to beat. His breath left his body. He rushed to the door and opened it a crack. Hands shaking while still holding the door.

Two officers. White. Stiff faces.

"Your father in son?'

“He’s – yeah. But he’s asleep”

“Mind if we step in?”

In his mind Lamar wanted to shout no go away but what could Lamar do? So he opened the door wider.

They scanned the place like they were looking for a bomb.

“Had reports of drug activity in the building” one said. “You know anything about that?”

Lamar shook his head quickly.
The officer stared at him a little too long “You sure?”

“He said no” his dad snapped suddenly pushing himself off the couch, hair wild and eyes bloodshot. “We’re not fuckin selling anything, all right?”

“Watch your tone”.

“This is harassment” his dad spat. “Every month you come knocking like we’re dealers. I bet you don’t do that to the white folkes a few blocks down.”
Lamar’s heart pounded. His fingers dug into his palms.

The police didn't reply. Just handed him a card and walked out.

That night, Lamar walked into the kitchen, opened the fridge again – empty, except for ketchup and a tub of mouldy rice. He shut it.

He start to walk back to his room.

He looked around the living room, trying to remember the last time it was cleaned and smelling nice.

He got to his room and shut the door.
Lamar climbed onto the bed and started to cry.

Not the normal crying he does sometimes late at night when thinking of old memories. No, this was proper crying.

He really needed a hug like in that photo that he now placed on his table next to his bed.
He just needed to talk to someone. Anyone.
But instead he wasn't hiding anything and just let it go.

CHAPTER 6

The next morning, Lamar didn't even make it to class. He was already scheduled for isolation – three days.
It was the punishment for what happened earlier that week. This is how it went down.
Lamar sat in the tiny room at the back of school, arms folded, staring at the white wall in front of him. They called it Reflection Time, but really it was punishment.

"Why do you think you're here, Lamar?" Mr. Watkins asked from the desk.

Lamar didn't answer.

Because Jake threw a pen at him in class. Because Lamar finally snapped and told him to shut up or because when a black boy raises his voice, people get scared.

"Just think about your actions, yeah?" the teacher said, flipping through a folder without looking up.

Lamar thought about the cold flat waiting for him. The silence. The ache in his belly.
He didn't say a word.
He walked back home after the talk at school. The flat was quiet when he got home.
Too quiet.

"Dad?" he called, half-hoping for no answer. No groaning, no cursing, no beer cans rolling across the floor.
Nothing.
He checked the living room. Sofa empty. No note.
The bathroom. Empty.
He opened the wardrobe. Half the clothes were gone.
Lamar's chest tightened.

He stood still for a long time, just listening. Waiting for a response. Something telling him that his dad didn't just leave.
He went to the kitchen, grabbed a tin of beans, heated it on the stove. Ate it straight out the pan with a fork.

CHAPTER 7

After his three days of isolation that actually passed quite quickly he went back to school. Late as always but while he was running to school, he thought about where his dad could have gone as its been three days now. It wasn't his longest streak of being away from home.
The longest he has been away from home has to be a week and nothing compares to that. But when he left he also left a note on the counter for Lamar and for his mom.

This time nothing.

That's what made it ten times scarier.

As Lamar got into school he dragged himself to registration. Miss Henry stepped out of her classroom when she saw him walk past.

"Hey," she said gently. "Can I talk to you for a sec? Come on in."

He stopped.

"I heard you were in isolation. You okay?" He nodded. Barely.

She glanced down, then reached into her drawer. Pulled out a protein bar.
"Not much, but... take it."

He hesitated. Then took it.

Their eyes met—briefly. Something passed between them.

Not pity. Not charity. Just... kindness. Something Lamar hadn't felt in a long time.

"Thanks," he mumbled, and walked off before he said anything more.

CHAPTER 8

Lamar was halfway through a sandwich of stale bread and half-melted cheese when the knock came. Three quick raps on the door, like they were trying to break it down.

He froze.

His throat went dry. No way.
He'd hoped it wouldn't happen again—not so soon, not this time.

The door banged again.

Lamar was already standing. He wanted to run. Just run far away. But he was stuck - stuck in this house, in this life. He didn't even want to face his dad, but Lamar knew if he didn't open the door, they'd kick it in anyway.
His dad, barely conscious on the couch, let out a low moan, but didn't move. His last bottle of beer was half-full by his side, like it had become a part of him. Lamar

wiped his hands on his pants and walked toward the door. When he opened it, two police officers stood there, their faces were hard.

"Is your father home?" one of them asked, their eyes scanning the room with no care for how it looked.

Lamar didn't speak at first. He couldn't. He knew what they were here for.

"I asked if your father's here," the officer repeated.

Lamar swallowed. His words felt like they were stuck in his throat.

"Yeah... he's in there," he finally said, nodding toward the living room.

The officer stepped past him, like Lamar wasn't even there.

He could feel the man's eyes on him, cold, assessing, judging.

The other officer stayed in the doorway, looking at Lamar with the kind of stare that made him feel like he was already guilty of something.

"Is this your father's residence?" the officer asked, holding up a card with his dad's name on it.

Lamar nodded. He didn't know what to say.

"We've had reports of illegal substances being sold in this building. You're aware of that, right?"

The words hit him like a punch. His heart was beating too fast. Too loud.

"No," Lamar said, quickly. "No, I don't know anything about that."
The officer raised an eyebrow, his expression skeptical. "We'll need to check."

Lamar wanted to scream. He wanted to break down right there. But all he could do was stand in the doorway and watch them invade his life. They walked into the living room, barely sparing a glance at Lamar. He didn't follow them in.

He didn't want to see it.

"You're gonna have to leave," his dad suddenly slurred from the couch, voice ragged and thick with alcohol. "This is harassment, man. You can't just come in here like this."
The officers didn't flinch. One of them stood with his arms crossed, the other rifling through the room, checking every corner, under the couch cushions, pulling things off shelves.

One of them glanced back at Lamar, who was still standing in the doorway. His palms were sweating, his stomach tight.

"You sure about that? You sure you don't know what's going on in this house?"

Lamar opened his mouth to protest, but the words died before they could leave his lips. He felt small, invisible—like nothing he said would make a difference anyway. They'd already decided.

"We'll be back," the officer said, turning on his heel. "Next time, we won't be as nice."

CHAPTER 9

Lamar woke up the next morning to an empty apartment. His dad was gone, probably still out trying to find his next fix, and his mum was nowhere to be found either. Probably off with another guy, another night of partying and forgetting her son existed.

Lamar didn't even feel like trying to make it to school. He didn't feel like facing the hallway full of snickers, didn't feel like sitting through lessons that meant nothing. He had bigger things to deal with – things he couldn't explain to anyone.

He pulled his jacket on, zipped it up tight, and slipped out of the door.

It wasn't that he wanted to skip school – it was just that nothing felt worth the effort anymore.

The laughter, the looks, the whispers that followed him wherever he went – it was all too much.

The isolation room at school felt better than being out there, surrounded by kids who had no idea what it was like to wake up in a house that smelled like rotten food and desperation.

Lamar walked aimlessly through the city, past the closed shops and quiet streets.
His shoes made a hollow sound against the cracked pavement. The world around him seemed too loud, too bright, and too full of people who didn't know he existed.
He went to the park, sat down by the empty swings, and stared at the sky.
There was nothing. Just emptiness.

CHAPTER 10

It was late when Lamar returned home. He pushed open the door slowly, the place still dark. He didn't want to make noise. Didn't want anyone to notice him.

But then he heard it. His mum.

Her voice was shaking, like she was trying to hold it together but couldn't.

"I can't keep doing this. I can't… I'm so damn tired, Lamar."

Lamar froze.

He hadn't heard her like this before—weak, broken, vulnerable.

She wasn't shouting or swearing, wasn't drunk or high. Just… tired.

He peeked around the corner, saw her sitting on the kitchen floor, her face buried in her hands. The phone she'd been holding was on the ground beside her.

"Mum?" he whispered, his voice shaking.

She looked up at him, her eyes red, and for a second, Lamar saw his mother for the first time in a long while. She wasn't the strong woman who pretended everything was fine anymore.

She was just... a person, struggling.

"I... I'm sorry, baby," she said, her voice breaking. "I don't know how to fix any of this."

Lamar didn't know what to say.

He wanted to say something comforting.

Wanted to reach out and tell her everything would be okay, but he knew better.

Nothing was okay. Nothing had been okay for a long time.

Instead, he sat down next to her, not saying anything. Just... being there.

CHAPTER 11

The next day at school, Jake found him again.
Lamar was walking down the hallway, trying to avoid eye contact, trying to keep his head down. He didn't want trouble today.
But Jake wasn't letting up.

"Where's your crackhead dad, Lamar?" Jake sneered, blocking his path.
Lamar didn't say anything. He just kept his eyes on the floor, hoping Jake would get bored.

But Jake wasn't done. He shoved Lamar hard into the lockers.
Lamar hit the cold metal with a sickening thud.
His back flared with pain, and the breath was knocked out of him.
He barely had time to recover before Jake shoved him again, this time with enough force to knock him to the ground.

"Pathetic little son of a bitch," Jake muttered, standing over him.

The other kids circled around, laughing.

Some pulled out their phones and started to record.

Lamar just lay there. Didn't try to fight back, didn't shout or scream. He couldn't. He didn't have it in him anymore.

CHAPTER 12

By the end of the day, Lamar's head was spinning. The pain in his back was a dull ache, the bruises still fresh on his skin.

He tried to leave school without anyone noticing, but of course, Miss Henry caught him at the door.

"Lamar," she said, her voice soft but insistent. "Come here."

He turned slowly, looking at the floor, wishing he could just disappear. She stepped closer, her eyes scanning him carefully.

"What happened to you?" she asked quietly.

He flinched, but didn't answer.

"I'm not going to tell anyone." She added, her voice gentle. "But you need to talk to someone. You don't have to do this alone."

Lamar opened his mouth to say something, but the words didn't come out.

Instead, he just turned away, walking out of the school without another word.

CHAPTER 13

That night, after his mum had fallen asleep on the couch, Lamar sat up in his room, staring at the cracked ceiling.

His stomach growled, but there was nothing to eat.

His dad was gone now longer than before and his mum didn't care, and he was stuck in this cycle that never seemed to end.

The world outside was still, the city's low hum just a distant buzz. And for the first time

Lamar realised something.

He wasn't sure how much longer he could take it.

CHAPTER 14

Lamar had a hard night with all these emotions going through his brain.
He got up and went to the kitchen to get some water to refresh him and ended up sleeping on the couch.
Lamar was half asleep on the couch when the knock came. It wasn't the normal knock. It was sharp, insistent. He knew it was them before he even got up to answer. He could feel it in his bones.

The officers were back.

He opened the door slowly. His stomach twisted with dread. Lamar was still half asleep as it was six in the morning now.

"Lamar Brown?"one of the officers asked, looking down at him like he was nothing but trouble.

"Yeah?" Lamar croaked, trying to sound like he wasn't already defeated.

"We need to ask you a few questions," the officer said, voice cold and flat.

"About your father."

Lamar's heart slammed in his chest.

He hadn't seen his dad in days—maybe a week, but it wasn't like he cared.

His dad was a ghost, just another shadow in this broken house.

Before Lamar could say anything, the officer took another step closer, his hand brushing the gun holstered on his belt.

Lamar's breath caught.

The officer's partner stood further back, watching him, eyes narrowed.

"What's going on?" Lamar's voice was barely above a whisper. His mind was racing.

Were they accusing him of something?

"We think your father fled the city. He's under investigation for dealing drugs, and we believe you know more than you're letting on," the officer said, his tone like a blade.

Lamar's stomach dropped.
His dad?
A drug dealer?
Wasn't that obvious?

He'd seen him high too many times to count. But Lamar couldn't tell them anything—his father was gone, and Lamar wasn't about to give them any more of his life.

Before he could respond, the officer moved in closer. Lamar stepped back instinctively.
"Where is he?" the officer pressed.
"I don't know," Lamar answered, his voice shaking. "I haven't seen him."

The officer stepped into the house, blocking Lamar's escape, and then the air shifted—Lamar could feel it. Something was wrong.

"Don't lie to me boy," the officer snapped, his eyes dark with anger.

Lamar's pulse was in his throat.

He took a step back, his heart pounding harder.

His back was against the wall.

The officer's hand went to his holster—too quickly.

Lamar's eyes locked on the gun.

A cold sweat broke out on the back of his neck as he stared at the officer.

The gun was pointed in his direction.

Everything seemed to slow down.

"Wait! I told you, I don't know where he is!" Lamar shouted, his voice breaking, a panic gripping his chest.

He could barely breathe.

The gun was too close.

The officer's partner didn't even flinch. They were treating him like a criminal already.

Shit. This isn't happening.

"You're just a kid," the officer muttered.

"But you're still guilty by association."

Lamar's legs felt like they were going to give out. He was stuck—trapped in a place where there was no way out.

The officer kept his eyes on Lamar for a long second, his finger hovering over the trigger. Then he spoke, his voice low, threatening.

"Next time, we won't be so nice."

They left just as fast as they'd come.

Lamar stayed frozen in the doorway, the weight of the gun in his mind heavy, suffocating.

CHAPTER 15

Lamar didn't know what to do. He didn't know if he should even move from where he was standing.

His hands was still trembling. He looked at it like it wasn't even his. His whole body was shaking.

The gun. The officer's face.

The way they looked at him – like he was just another suspect, just another name on a list of kids who didn't matter.

The sound of the door slamming shut echoed in his head.
It wouldn't stop.
His chest felt tight. Too tight.
He finally forced himself to move.
Slowly, he crossed the room to the couch.
His dad wasn't coming back.
And the cops didn't care about him.

They cared about his father and whether or not Lamar had something to do with the mess his dad had made.
He sat down hard on the couch, the rough fabric pressing into his skin.
He stared at the empty space in the corner of the room—the spot where his dad had passed out too many times. The smell of stale beer and sweat still lingered in the air. He didn't know how long he sat there. Maybe an hour. Maybe two.
The whole time, he kept hearing the officer's voice, telling him he was guilty. He could feel the weight of the gun aimed at him.

Just a kid, they said. Like that made a difference.

Lamar's eyes burned. He hadn't properly cried in a long time.
Not since he was younger like that time he broke his arm playing football.

But now, sitting in the same broken place, he felt like it was all coming down on him. His heart was breaking, his chest tightening. He couldn't breathe.

When his mum came in later, she didn't ask where he'd been.
She didn't ask if he was okay.

She didn't ask anything. She just dropped a bag of fast food on the table and sat down in the chair.

For a second, Lamar thought maybe she'd say something.

Maybe she'd notice the way his hands were shaking. Maybe she'd ask why he looked like he'd just seen a ghost.

But no.

She didn't look at him. She didn't look at anything.
He didn't know how to say it.
He didn't know how to say that the world was closing in on him, that the police had almost shot him, that he didn't know where his dad was, or if his life would ever feel safe again.
Instead, he just sat there, staring at the food she had brought home.
His stomach growled, but it didn't feel like it belonged to him.

CHAPTER 16

By the time Lamar walked into school the next day, it felt like he was carrying a weight in his chest—a heavy, suffocating weight that made everything around him blur. He wasn't ready to face the world.

The hallways were loud. The other students didn't notice him as he shuffled through the crowd, head down, trying to stay invisible. It wasn't hard. They didn't look at him.

The only person who did was Miss Henry. She was standing near the lockers when Lamar walked past, and for the first time in a long while she didn't say anything. She just watched him for a second, like she knew something wasn't right.

"You okay, Lamar?" she asked, her voice soft but firm.

Lamar stopped dead in his tracks.

He wanted to tell her everything—wanted to break down and scream—but all he could do was shake his head.

He didn't have the strength for it. Not right now.

"I'm fine," he lied.

But she wasn't buying it.

Miss Henry's eyes softened, and for a brief moment, Lamar thought he might see her crack too.
But she didn't. She just nodded slowly, like she knew there was more to the story than he was saying.

"All right," she said, her voice quiet. "If you need to talk..."

He didn't respond. He didn't know what he needed.

But he wasn't going to talk about it. Not yet. Not to her. Not to anyone.

CHAPTER 17

Lamar was walking on thin ice.

He could feel it under his feet every time he stepped outside, every time he faced the walls of his house, every time he had to see the faces of the people at school.

He couldn't escape it – the pressure, the pain, the weight.

It was like the world was slowly crushing him, bit by bit, until he couldn't
breathe anymore.

Every day felt like a struggle for survival.
His bruises were fading, but the memories of what happened with the cops – of the gun being pulled on him – were still fresh in his mind.
And the bullying at school didn't help. It had been getting worse. They were starting to get physical now. Jake, the guy who'd been tormenting him, was relentless.

Lamar tried to tell himself it wasn't worth it. That he could handle it. But every shove, every name, every whispered slur was like a knife twisting deeper into his chest. It was suffocating.

And his parents?

Well, his dad was still gone, doing whatever he was doing,

And his mum?

She wasn't even there anymore, not in the way she was supposed to be. She was too lost in her own world of partying and escaping to notice Lamar.

The nights were the worst.

Lamar would lie awake in his room, staring at the cracked ceiling, his mind spinning with thoughts he couldn't control.

He couldn't escape them.

He couldn't outrun them.

One night, he stood in front of the mirror, staring at his reflection.

His eyes were bloodshot, his skin pale.

He barely recognised the boy staring back at him.

Was this what his life had become?

Lamar wanted to scream.

He wanted to tear down the walls and shout at the world that he wasn't just some kid to be ignored, some problem to be solved. But all he could do was stand there in silence, feeling more invisible than ever.

CHAPTER 18

The next morning, Miss Henry noticed him again.

Lamar was sitting in the back of the class, trying to disappear into the corner.

But Miss Henry always saw through his walls.

"Lamar," she said softly, her eyes meeting his. "Can I talk to you after class?"
Lamar froze.
He wanted to say no, wanted to tell her that everything was fine, but the words wouldn't come.

He couldn't lie to her anymore.

Not after everything that had happened.

After class, he lingered by the door, hesitating.

Finally, Miss Henry approached him, her face full of concern.
"Are you sure you're okay?" she asked gently. "You don't look well."

Lamar opened his mouth to brush it off, but then something snapped. The emotions he'd been holding in for so long broke through all at once.

"I'm not okay," he whispered, his voice barely audible. "I'm not okay, Miss Henry. Everything is… everything is falling apart. I don't know what to do anymore."

The words came out in a rush, faster than he could stop them. He felt the tears start to sting his eyes, but he quickly wiped them away, trying to hold it together.

Miss Henry didn't say anything for a long time. She just stood there, letting him speak.

Finally, she put a hand on his shoulder. "You don't have to go through this alone, Lamar. There are people who can help you. You're not invisible. You're not nothing."
Lamar felt a strange warmth spread through him at her words.

It was the first time in a long while that anyone had made him feel like he mattered.

"I don't know who to talk to," Lamar muttered. "My dad's gone, and my mum doesn't care. The kids at school just... they just make everything worse. I don't know how to get out of it."

Miss Henry looked at him, her eyes full of empathy. "You're not alone, Lamar. I promise you. I know it's hard, but you don't have to carry this by yourself."

But Lamar wasn't ready to let anyone in. Not yet. "I'll be fine," he said quickly, stepping back from her.

CHAPTER 19

The bullying escalated in a way Lamar hadn't expected. Jake and the others were relentless now. It wasn't just name-calling.

They were slapping his books out of his hands, tripping him in the hallways, and laughing as they watched him struggle to pick everything up.

It didn't matter that Lamar was already a mess inside; to them, he was just an easy target.

Lamar tried to stand tall, to ignore them, but each insult, each shove, was like a crack in his armour. And every day, it got harder to keep the pieces of himself together.

One day, after school, it went too far. Jake pushed him into the lockers again, and this time, Lamar didn't take it. He snapped.

"Leave me the fuck alone!" Lamar screamed, his voice breaking, his fists clenched.

Jake stopped, his smirk turning into a frown.

For a second, Lamar thought maybe the bullying would stop.

But then Jake shoved him again, harder this time.
"What's the matter, Lamar? You gonna cry like a little bitch?"
And that was it.

Lamar swung. It wasn't planned. It was a blur of movement, anger, and frustration. He hit Jake hard in the face, feeling the sickening crunch of bone under his knuckles.
The hallway went quiet. Jake stumbled back, blood trickling from his nose. He looked at Lamar with wide eyes, shocked.

For a split second, Lamar felt powerful.

For a split second, he felt like he'd taken control of his life.

But then the realisation hit him. The tears in his eyes blurred his vision.
The fight didn't end there. Jake shoved Lamar against the lockers again, and this time, a teacher came running. They both got sent to the principal's office.

CHAPTER 20

By the time Lamar got home, the guilt had already started to eat him alive.

The fight with Jake had been a turning point, but it wasn't the kind of victory Lamar had hoped for.

It had only made things worse.

Now he was in trouble, and the humiliation felt like it was choking him.

His mum was passed out on the couch again, the TV blaring some reality show. She hadn't even noticed him walk in.

The words Miss Henry had said to him echoed in his head,

You don't have to go through this alone.

But it felt like everyone was ignoring him.

Like he was invisible, a ghost in his own home.

He sat on the floor, staring at the wall, the weight of everything pressing down on him. His heart was heavy, and his mind was too full. The whole world seemed to be crashing down around him, and there was nowhere to turn.

The phone rang, breaking the silence. He didn't even look at it.
It was probably the school, calling to tell his mom about the fight. It didn't matter.

Nothing mattered anymore.

CHAPTER 21

The days dragged on, and Lamar sank deeper into the numbness.

He wasn't sleeping well.

His mind wouldn't shut off.

The weight of the trauma – the bullying, the police, the absence of his dad – kept him locked in a cage of fear and isolation.

He couldn't even focus on school anymore. His grades slipped further, and the fights with Jake didn't help. Every day felt like a battle he couldn't win.

He didn't know how much longer he could keep pretending to be okay.

CHAPTER 22

Finally, after a week of barely functioning, Lamar found himself back in Miss Henry's classroom.

He hadn't planned on talking to her.

He hadn't planned on talking to anyone.

But when he sat down at his desk, Miss Henry walked over to him, her face full of concern.

"Lamar," she said gently.

"Have you thought about talking to someone about what's going on? You don't have to do this alone."

Lamar met her gaze. For the first time in a long time, he didn't feel like running away.

He felt... safe. Just for a moment.

"I don't know if I can," he said quietly. "But... maybe I should."

Miss Henry helped Lamar get in touch with a counsellor at the school.

It wasn't much, but it was a start. It was a way out of the darkness, even if Lamar didn't know what it would lead to.

Lamar's sessions with the counsellor weren't easy.
He didn't open up right away.
But little by little, he started to talk about the things that haunted him—the bullying, the fear of the police, his broken family.
It wasn't a quick fix. It wasn't a magic solution. But it was something.
He still had a long way to go, but Lamar wasn't as alone as he used to be. He had people who cared, people who were ready to listen. That was a start.

CHAPTER 23

It didn't happen overnight. But by the end of the year Lamar had started to change.

It wasn't easy.

He still had his bad days.

The trauma was still there.

The bullying didn't stop completely.

But Lamar was stronger now. He had tools to cope, people he could lean on, and a future that didn't seem as dark.

And as he walked out of school that day, Lamar felt something he hadn't felt in a long time – hope.

EPILOGUE

A Message for You

If you're reading this, and you've ever felt like Lamar – alone, lost, invisible – remember this:

You're not alone

No matter how dark it feels, no matter how heavy the weight on your chest, there is always someone who cares. There's always help. Never be afraid to reach out. Your voice matters.

You matter

To the Adults, Parents, Teachers. Check in. Ask twice. Be the reason someone feels seen.

Because sometimes, the difference between sinking and surviving is someone caring enough to ask "Are you okay?"

Printed in Great Britain
by Amazon

62262921R00037